SILENT SARGE

GOOD GOLLY! IT'S GOTTEN WORSE!!

I WANT YOU TO HELP SARGE GET TO A THROAT SPECIALIST IN TOWN

WE'VE GOT TO DO SOME-THING ABOUT THIS.
A SERGEANT WITHOUT A VOICE IS LIKE A LIGHT-HOUSE WITHOUT A FOG HORN

HE STILL CAN'T TALK?

I'VE MADE AN APPOINTMENT FOR YOU AT TWO P.M.

CARE TO GO FOR A SPIN, BOYS?

GEE, SARGE, IT MUST BE TOUGH FOR **YOU** TO HAVE LARYNGITIS
WOW, BEETLE, LOOK!
LOUIE'S USED CARS
SPECI
$1500

BOY! WOULD WE!

I'LL DRIVE!

VROOM
HEY!

WHAT A BUGGY!
LET 'ER GO!
OOPS! I FORGOT MY SALES BOOK.

COME BACK!

GOSH! THERE'S SARGE! I FORGOT ALL ABOUT HIM!
LOOK WHAT WE GOT, SARGE!

THOSE CRAZY IDIOTS COULD GET IN BAD TROUBLE

OMIGOSH!
THEY STOLE A CAR!!

HEY!
I'VE GOTTA RETURN THIS QUICK!

WONDER WHERE THEY PICKED IT UP!

YOU GOT TO ADMIRE HIM! HE'S SURE LOYAL TO HIS BUDDIES! WON'T TELL US A THING!

OKAY, MAC, WE GOT YOU! WHERE'S YOUR BUDDY?
POLICE

I'LL GET HIM TO TALK IF IT TAKES ALL DAY!
END

The
ENTERTAINER

A LADY TOOK HER HUSBAND TO THE DOCTOR. " HE THINKS HE'S A REFRIGERATOR," SHE SAID.

"THAT'S HARMLESS," SAID THE DOC.
"BUT WHEN HE SLEEPS WITH HIS MOUTH OPEN, THE LIGHT KEEPS ME AWAKE"

I'M GOOD AT IMITATIONS, TOO
AWRIGHT, YOUSE GUYS!!

HOW ABOUT A SONG?
LET ME ENTERTAIN YOU

LET ME MAKE YOU SMILE

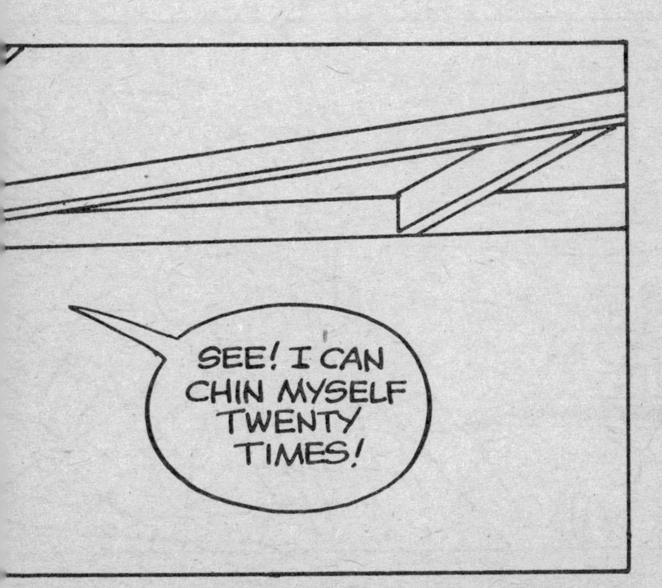
SEE! I CAN CHIN MYSELF TWENTY TIMES!

EVER SEE THIS?

BOO!

ALWAYS GOOD FOR A LAUGH!

LOOK! FUNNY FACE!

WE'RE BACK, BEETLE

AFTER A DAY OF FISHING TOGETHER THE SON SAID TO HIS DAD, "GEE I DIDN'T KNOW FISH TOOK DAYS OFF, TOO."

IT'S ABOUT TIME! I'VE HAD TO ENTERTAIN THE READERS ALL BY MYSELF!
END

The

SEARCH

WHERE DID HE GO?

I HAVEN'T SEEN HIM SINCE BREAKFAST, SARGE

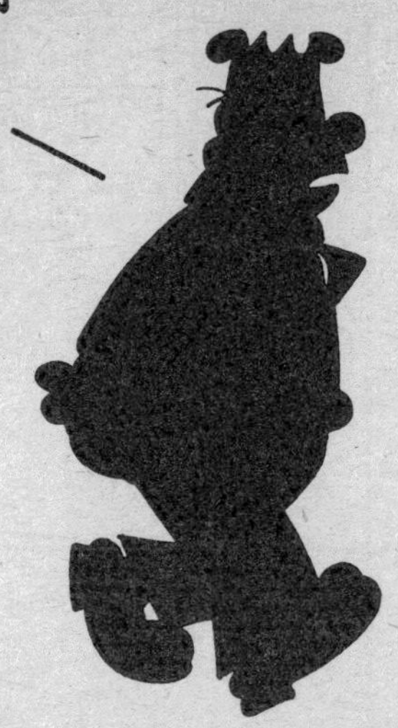
I HAVEN'T SEEN HIM SINCE I TOLD HIM I HAD A JOB FOR HIM

MAYBE HE'S AT THE OFFICE NOW

NOPE!

☆!!@# ~~
HE WAS SUPPOSED TO FILL THAT COAL BUCKET
I GUESS I'LL HAVE TO KEEP LOOKING FOR HIM

LET'S SEE-- IF I WERE BEETLE I'D BE GRABBING A NAP ON THE LAUNDRY BAGS

OR SIPPING A SODA BEHIND THE JUKE BOX IN THE PX

OR SAMPLING A PIE IN THE STORE-ROOM

WELL, I GUESS HE SNEAKED OFF TO TOWN FOR DINNER WITH HIS GIRL

BEETLE! WHAT ARE YOU DOING SCRUNCHED DOWN IN A DIRTY CORNER OF THE COAL BIN?

BOY! I WISH I WERE YOU, BEETLE. WHAT A TIME I'D HAVE HAD TODAY

PICKY
INSPECTOR

DUST THOSE CORNERS... IRON YOUR SHOELACES...

INSPECTION IN TWENTY MINUTES!!

YOU TOO, BEETLE! GET YOUR STUFF READY FOR INSPECTION!
YEAH! YOU KNOW HOW TOUGH SARGE IS!

HOW ABOUT THOSE CANDY BARS IN YOUR GAS MASK?
HE'LL NEVER FIND THEM! HOW ABOUT THAT CAKE IN YOUR KNAPSACK?

I WAS DOING A GOOD JOB OF FORGETTING ABOUT IT UNTIL YOU HAD TO REMIND ME OF IT!

HIDE THESE BOTTLES IN YOUR BOOTS, WILL YA?

GET READY, EVERYONE
HERE COMES
TROUBLE!

TEN-
SHUN!
YOU HAVE RING AROUND
THE COLLAR, MILLER.
TWO
DEMERITS

RUST ON BAKER'S RIFLE-- TWO DEMERITS!
CANDY IN BEETLE'S GAS MASK--SIX DEMERITS

CLEAN OUT YOUR FOOT LOCKER-- FOUR DEMERITS

GUM UNDER TOMPKINS' BED--TWO DEMERITS

CAKE IN KILLER'S KNAPSACK--FOUR DEMERITS

DUST UNDER FOSTER'S SHOES --ONE DEMERIT
HARPER'S RIFLE BELT IS BROKEN --TWO DEMERITS

GET THOSE BOTTLES OUT OF YOUR BOOTS, JOSLIN--TWO DEMERITS
MISSING BUTTON, CALLOWAY-- ONE DEMERIT

EVERYONE RESTRICTED TO BARRACKS FOR ONE HOUR
SLAM

GEE! HE MUST HAVE X-RAY EYES!
HE JUST WALKED THROUGH AND FOUND EVERYTHING
IT MUST COME WITH YEARS OF EXPERIENCE

AW!

HE'S SHREWD ALL RIGHT!
OH, HE'S NOT SO SHREWD! HE MISSED THE BANANA IN MY BED-ROLL

BANANA IN BED-ROLL --THREE DEMERITS
END

DIRECT

ORDERS

OUR SCOUT REPORTS THAT THE BLUE ARMY IS FORMING TO ATTACK OUR RIGHT FLANK, SIR

I'D BETTER TAKE A LOOK AND SEE HOW HE INTENDS TO PROTECT THAT FLANK

OH, NO!...GIVE ME THAT. I WANT TO TALK TO LT. FUZZ

HURRUMPH...
THIS IS GENERAL
HALFTRACK
ULP!
YES,
SIR!

FORM IN A SKIRMISH
LINE ON THE ROAD--

NOW SIT THERE AND AWAIT FURTHER ORDERS

GO STRAIGHT SOUTH ON THE ROAD AHEAD OF YOU TILL YOU COME TO A BRIDGE--

SIR! CAN YOU TELL ME HOW TO GET TO THE GEM HOTEL IN POTTSVILLE?

TURN RIGHT AT THE BRIDGE FOR TWO MILES --THEN LEFT AT THE STOP LIGHT

GO PAST THE DAIRY FARM. TURN RIGHT ON THE HIGHWAY ---

GO TELL THE MANAGER **HELLO** FOR ME -- HE'S AN OLD FRIEND OF MINE
I WILL

STAY ON THAT ROAD AND YOU'LL COME OUT ON MAIN STREET-- HALF WAY DOWN YOU'LL FIND THE **GEM HOTEL**
THANK YOU

WHAT'S GOING ON?!! SOLDIERS KEEP POURING IN AND SAYING **HELLO** TO ME!
END

SNACK
ATTACK

ZZZ HUH!!? WHAZZIT?
RUMBLE
GROAN
K-CHOOM

OH, IT'S **YOU** WANTING TO BE FED AGAIN!
RUMBLE
ACK-ACK
PHOOM!

EMPTY! I'LL BE AWAKE ALL NIGHT IF I DON'T GET SOMETHING TO EAT!
CHIPS
GROANNN

HEY! HE FORGOT TO LOCK THE DOOR! WHAT A BREAK!
AND SOMEONE LEFT THE KITCHEN LIGHT ON
MESS HALL

COOKIE SAID HE'D KILL ANYBODY WHO'D BREAK IN HERE AFTER HOURS, BUT THIS IS FOR THE GOOD OF OUR OUTFIT
MESS HALL

COOKIE'S ALWAYS GROUSING ABOUT ME COMING AROUND FOR FOOD, BUT THIS TIME HE WON'T--

WUP!
KP

THERE'S THE GUY I WAS TELLING YOU ABOUT, HONEY!
END

"OUT of UNIFORM"
I WISH I HAD THE BRAINS TO BE AN OFFICER!

IT DOESN'T TAKE BRAINS! IT'S ALL IN THE UNIFORM!
THAT'S RIGHT!

WATCH -- I'LL SHOW YOU!

A COUPLE OF STARS ON MY HELMET, SOME BRASS, A SCARF --

PUT ON MY DARK GLASSES
AND PUT A CIGAR IN YOUR MOUTH
HERE'S A HOLSTER

HE LOOKS SO MUCH LIKE AN OFFICER I WANT TO KICK HIM!

WHAT A SORRY-LOOKING SPECIMAN -- IF YOU CAN CALL IT A MAN!

WHAT'S GOING ON HERE?
TEN-SHUN!

HO! HO! HO! GEE! BEETLE SURE HAS HIM FOOLED!

AW! WHY DID YOU HAVE TO TELL HIM?

BEETLE!!

I'LL HAVE YOU COURT-MARTIALED FOR IMPERSONATING AN OFFICER

YOU THINK HE LOOKS LIKE AN **OFFICER?!** RIDICULOUS!
US

LET THAT BE A LESSON TO YOU!

I SHOULD HAVE YOU COURT-MARTIALED FOR SLANDER!

THESE ENLISTED MEN DRIVE ME NUTS!
OFFICER'S CLUB

COLONEL, SOMETIMES I WONDER WHERE THESE G.I.'S GET THEIR IDEAS!

END

BEETLE Takes

the CAKE!

HEY! HE'S TRYING TO SNEAK OFF WITHOUT SHARING IT!

STOP HIM!

OH, OH... HERE THEY COME!
IF THEY THINK THEY'RE GOING TO GET SOME OF THIS CAKE THEY'RE NUTS!

MY GIRL MADE THIS FOR MY BIRTHDAY AND IT'S ALL MINE!
ZZZ

WHAT THE--

HE JUMPED OUT THIS WINDOW
I DON'T SEE HIM

WHERE IS HE?
THERE HE GOES!!

NOW WHERE'S THAT MESSENGER WITH THE NEW MINE THEY DEVELOPED AT THE PROVING GROUNDS?
IT HAS TO BE ON THE PLANE FOR WASHINGTON IN TEN MINUTES
US

GIVE ME THAT! I'LL JUST MAKE THE PLANE!

SO **THAT'S** THE NEW SECRET WEAPON?
Y'KNOW, IT LOOKS SORTA LIKE A CAKE
IT'S HARD AS A ROCK!

WELL, LET'S GET BUSY AND SEE HOW QUICK WE CAN TURN OUT A MILLION OF THEM
US
US
END

BEETLE'S

MELON

NO ONE'S EVER ASKED ME THAT BEFORE!

I WOULDN'T MIND A FEW WATERMELONS. I WONDER IF THERE'S ANY RULE OR REGULATION AGAINST IT?
US

I LIKE WATERMELONS BUT I'D BETTER GET THE CAPTAIN'S PERMISSION

WE COULD LOOK IN THE ARMY REGULATIONS

"GOVERNMENT PROPERTY SHALL NOT BE CHANGED, DIVERTED, OR USED IN ANY WAY FOR PRIVATE PURPOSES"

BUT IT SAYS HERE "ATTEMPTS SHALL BE MADE TO BEAUTIFY THE MILITARY RESERVE
HMMMM

WE'D BETTER GET THE MAJOR TO DECIDE ON THIS
US

A WATERMELON PATCH?
US

IT SEEMS LIKE A GREAT IDEA--BUT ON THE OTHER HAND--

I CAN SEE IT NOW! WATER-MELONS ALL OVER THE PLACE
WHY DO THESE PROBLEMS HAVE TO COME UP?
YOUR CALL TO WASHINGTON IS THROUGH, GENERAL
US
US

WHAT I'D LIKE TO KNOW IS WHO'S GOING TO HARVEST ALL THESE WATERMELONS?
WE OUGHT TO LET THE GENERAL IN ON THIS

THE CHIEF SAYS IT'S OKAY TO GO AHEAD WITH THE "WATERMELON FARM PROJECT"

SOMEHOW ALL THE JOY IS GONE OUT OF IT!
END

TOY BOY
WAY
WHERE ?

COME ON, KILLER WE'VE GOT AN HOUR TO KILL. LET'S BROWSE AROUND IN PEEBLE'S DEPARTMENT STORE!

WHERE? IN THE TOY DEPARTMENT OF COURSE!

GEE, I ALWAYS WANTED ONE OF THESE WHEN I WAS A KID!
CAREFUL! DON'T BREAK ANYTHING!

YOU KNOW HOW CLUMSY YOU ARE, BEETLE

THAT'S FUNNY! I CAN'T GET MY FEET OUT!
I KNEW IT!
FIRE DE

DO YOU WISH TO PURCHASE THAT TRUCK, SIR?

I'M SORRY ABOUT ALL THIS CON-FUSION IN MY DEPARTMENT, SIR
I SHOULD NEVER HAVE TAKEN YOU OUT OF THE BOOK DEPARTMENT, MISS FROBUSH

I JUST WISH TO GET OUT OF IT! I'M STUCK!
WHAT'S THIS?
FIRE DEPT.

HOLD IT!
HOW CAN I DO ANYTHING ELSE?
FIRE DEPT.
DON'T SCRATCH THE MERCHANDISE!

WILL SOMEBODY GET ME OUT OF THIS THING!!?

HMMM
HMMM
HMMM

BEFORE WE REMOVE HIM WE MUST BE SURE WE ARE PROTECTED

HERE ARE THE RELEASE FORMS YOU WANTED FROM THE LEGAL DEPARTMENT

SIGN THERE! IT SAYS THE STORE ISN'T RESPONSIBLE FOR DAMAGES SUCH AS LOSS OF LIMBS
HE SIGNED IT!
FIRE D

YES...I'LL BE UP IN A JIFFY

GET THE HANDYMAN UP HERE WITH A CROWBAR AND SLEDGE HAMMER!

OOF! HE'S REALLY STUCK!
EASY! DON'T BEND THE TRUCK!
FIRE DEPT.
POW!

MAYBE WE CAN SHAKE IT OFF!
FIRE DEPT.

CAN OPENER 59 CENTS
HOUSEHOLD GOODS

STOP!! I'LL BUY THE THING!
WE'LL GIVE YOU A $5 DISCOUNT FOR THE "DEFECT" IN IT!

I DON'T KNOW HOW MUCH LONGER I CAN AFFORD YOUR FRIENDSHIP
HEY! DID YOU NOTICE THIS BELL?!
DING DING
FIRE DEPT.
END

The Rain

Drips

I'M GROWING **MOSS** ON MY LEFT SIDE
YOU'RE **LUCKY!** I'M GETTING **BARNACLES!**

QUIET, EVERYBODY! I'M GETTING A WEATHER REPORT!

HEAVY RAIN CONTINUING THROUGH THE NIGHT AND ALL DAY TOMORROW...

I HOPE THAT'S ONE OF THOSE UNDERWATER PENS YOU'RE USING!
QUIET, YA DRIP! I'M WRITING TO MY GIRL!

WE SHOULDA DUG A TRENCH AROUND OUR TENT! WATER'S STARTING TO SEEP IN!
DON'T WORRY! THIS AIR MATTRESS WILL KEEP US **HIGH AND DRY!**

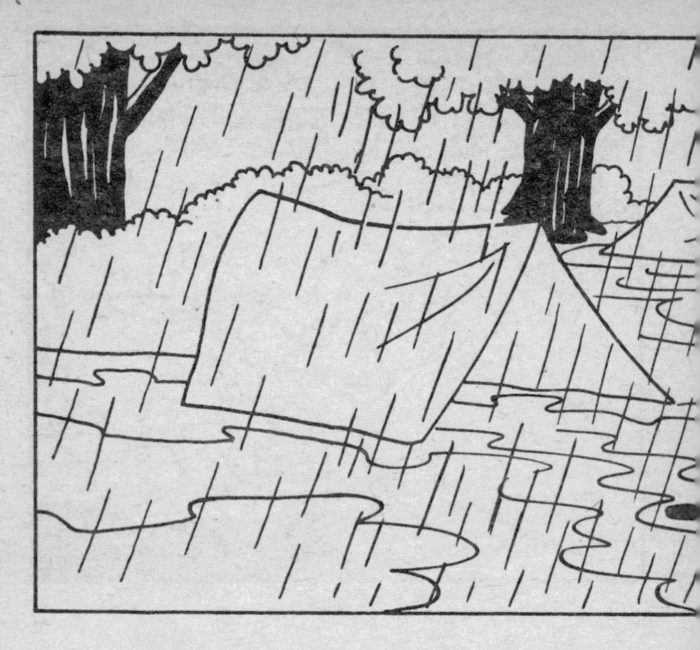

HOLY CATS! WE'RE REALLY MOVING!!

!
THAT'S FUNNY! I FEEL SEASICK ALL OF A SUDDEN!
SU

WELL, DON'T JUST SIT THERE. DO SOME-THING!
WHAT WOULD YOU LIKE? A SWAN DIVE? A HALF-GAINER?

CRACK

FOOEY! I CAN'T WRITE ANY MORE! GOT A STAMP?
YEAH, AND YOU DON'T EVEN HAVE TO LICK IT!

THERE GOES OUR **TENT!**
I HOPE THAT DIDN'T HURT MY LUCKY RABBIT'S FOOT I HAD HANGING INSIDE!

HELP ME ROW OVER TO THE MAIL TENT
"NEITHER STORM, NOR SNOW, NOR GLOOM OF NIGHT---"

Dear Bunny,
It's raining outside and I'm sitting here writing by candlelight...

CANDLELIGHT! ISN'T THAT ROMANTIC?!
---AND LOOK! TEARDROPS!
END

"PAPER WORK"

FOLLOW ME, BEETLE

I HAVE ANOTHER JOB FOR YOU

THAT BULLETIN BOARD NEEDS CLEANING OFF. TAKE EVERYTHING DOWN AND BRING IT IN TO ME

HEY! WHAT'S THIS?

YAHOOO!
PICK UP THOSE PAPERS, BAILEY!

PICK 'EM UP, YOURSELF! YOU FAT, LAZY SARGE!

HERE'S A SIZE-12 GUNBOAT SALUTE. I'VE BEEN SAVING FOR YOU SIR!

THIS IS ALL JUST A FANTASTIC DREAM

CALL THE GUARD, THE MARINES, THE WACS, THE K-9 CORPS!
PLOK

SOMEHOW THE SKY LOOKS BLUER-- THE GRASS GREENER

LET'S PLAY A NICE GAME, BEETLE
PRETEND YOU'RE A POT ROAST AND WE'LL TIE YOU UP WITH THIS STRING
OKAY, BUT YOU GUYS SHOULD READ THIS

CAREFUL, MEN. HE'S VIOLENT!

"MEN OF THIS COMPANY ARE RELEASED TO CIVILIAN STATUS AS OF TODAY" GEN. HILL NOV. 15, 1918"
1918!

THAT'S WHY I WANTED THE BULLETIN BOARD CLEANED OFF!

WELL, GUESS I'D BETTER GET OVER TO THE MESS HALL AND START ON THE DISHES
END

BEETLE and SARGE

VERY WELL. COME WITH ME, BEETLE

ELECTRIC FLOOR-SCRUBBER!! THAT'S AN ORDER!!!
A CO.

THERE. NOW YOU JUST KEEP HELPING US OUT UNTIL IT GETS HERE

THAT WAS ANOTHER WASTE OF MY TIME
END